dick bruna

miffy at the zoo

SIMON AND SCHUSTER
London New York Sydney Toronto New Delhi

One morning Miffy's daddy said

– we're going to the zoo.

I think you'll really love it.

There's lots to see and do.

The zoo, cried little Miffy,

oh, that will be just great!

But isn't it a long, long way?

I hope the train's not late.

And so they set off on the train

which went along so fast

that Miffy sat and watched the world

go swiftly speeding past.

They travelled for about an hour

till Daddy pointed, see?

We're there at last now, Miffy.

Come on, follow me.

At first they met the parrots

who perched along a walk.

The parrots cackled, hello Miff

in cheery parrot talk.

But look - what's that? cried Miffy,

that funny little horse!

A horse with stripes all over it.

A zebra? Yes, of course.

They also saw a kangaroo.

In front she had a pouch

for carrying her baby in

– a comfy tummy couch.

Next they saw an elephant.

Enormous, Miffy said,

and look, he's stretching out his trunk

to take a piece of bread.

And have you seen the monkey there,

swinging from a tree?

For monkeys, swinging with one hand

is easy as can be.

Now those giraffes, oh goodness me,

their necks reach up so high

but they won't hurt you, Miffy dear,

they won't make you cry.

To finish with, said Daddy,

Miffy, you decide.

She chose the giant tortoise

and had a lovely ride.

The day was nearly over now.

They got back on the train

and tired Miffy fell asleep

as they went home again.

Original title: nijntje in de dierentuin
Original text Dick Bruna © copyright Mercis Publishing bv, 1963
Illustrations Dick Bruna © copyright Mercis bv, 1963
This edition published in Great Britain in 2014 by Simon and Schuster UK Limited
1st Floor, 222 Gray's Inn Road, London WC1X 8HB, A CBS Company
Publication licensed by Mercis Publishing bv, Amsterdam
English re-translation by Tony Mitton © copyright 2014, based on the
original English translation of Patricia Crampton © copyright 1995
ISBN 978 1 4711 2082 4
Printed and bound in China
A CIP catalogue record for this book is available from the British Library upon request
10 9 8 7 6 5

www.simonandschuster.co.uk